I'll miss you Zeb! @ Ms. Hen

EZRA'S
WOOKIEE RESCUE
Read-Along
STORYBOOK AND CD

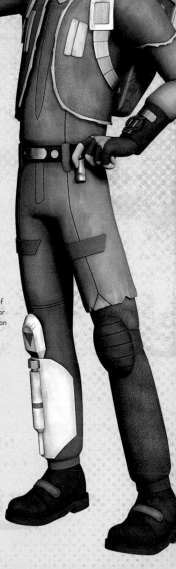

This is the story of a boy named Ezra, who was destined to join a daring group of rebels in their fight against the Empire. You can join their mission by reading along with me in your book. Just turn the page when you hear this sound. . . .

Let's begin now.

Printed in the United States of America

First Edition 1 3 5 7 9 10 8 6 4 2

Library of Congress Control Number: 2014937132

V381-8386-5-14248

ISBN 978-1-4847-0504-9

For more Disney Press fun, visit www.disneybooks.com

Visit the official Star Wars website at: www.starwars.com

SUSTAINABLE FORESTRY INITIATIVE
www.sfiprogram.org
SFI-00993

Certified Chain of Custody
At Least 20% Certified Forest Content

For Text Only

Disney
LUCASFILM
PRESS

Los Angeles • New York

It was a dark time in the galaxy. The Empire had defeated all the Jedi and taken control of many planets.

One planet under Imperial control was Lothal, a tiny farming world on the Outer Rim of the galaxy. A young boy named Ezra lived there. Ezra was used to Imperial troopers taking what they wanted from hardworking farmers.

But Ezra was also very clever. He knew ways to outwit the troops and take back the things they stole. Each day he'd bring extra supplies back to his secret tower home on the outskirts of Capital City.

Ezra didn't have any parents. He knew how to take care of himself. But he sometimes wondered what it would be like to have a real family.

One morning in the Lothal market, Ezra spotted two Imperial officers forcing the local vendors to give them supplies.

Behind the guards, several speeder bikes were stacked high with crates of stolen items. Ezra smiled sneakily. He was certain that if he timed things just right, he could snatch back some of the crates without them noticing!

Quietly, Ezra inched closer to the bikes. But before he could reach them, a tall man walked out from the crowd. Ezra stopped. A strange feeling came over him. "That was weird. . . ."

He didn't know the man, but for some reason, he felt like he was supposed to.

Ezra watched curiously as the man signaled to a girl in a helmet. The girl nodded and activated a remote detonator. Instantly, one of the speeder bikes burst into flames!

The market flew into a frenzy. Guards ran toward the explosion and attempted to move the supply bikes away from the disturbance. But their path was immediately blocked by the tall man. "How's it going?" The man smiled casually before pulling out a blaster and moving toward the loaded bikes.

He was joined by a gruff-looking alien, and together, the two quickly took down the remaining guards.

This was Ezra's chance! He leaped from his hiding spot right onto one of the loaded bikes. "Thanks for doing the heavy lifting!" He saluted the tall man before zipping away with the supplies.

"After that kid!" The man and the alien jumped on two nearby bikes and raced after Ezra.

Ezra managed to lose them on a busy street, but he wasn't as successful in shaking off the Imperial guards. Soon, Ezra was under fire from two speeder bikes and a trio of TIE fighters. "Whatever's in these crates must really be worth it!"

But Ezra couldn't dodge their blasts forever. A laser from one of the TIE fighters hit his bike, slowing the machine down to a crawl. Ezra leaped from the smoking bike and prepared himself for the worst. But just as the TIE was about to fire again, it exploded!

Ezra's eyes grew wide. A starship was swooping down toward him, and the tall man from the market was standing on the loading ramp. His ship had saved Ezra!

The man called to Ezra to jump aboard, but Ezra hesitated. "Kid, you have a better option?"

Gathering his courage, Ezra leaped onto the hovering spaceship, taking a supply crate with him.

On board the ship, the man and his companions introduced themselves. His name was Kanan, and he was their leader. The helmeted girl was Sabine. A Twi'lek woman called Hera piloted the ship—named the *Ghost*. A beat-up astromech droid named Chopper made all the ship's repairs. And the gruff-looking alien was Zeb.

Zeb was furious that Ezra had interfered with their mission. Ezra defended himself. "Look, I was just doing the same thing you were: stealing to survive!"

Zeb growled. "You have no idea what we were doing. You don't know us."

Hera landed the ship in a desolate part of Lothal. Refugees whose farms had been taken by the Empire streamed out from the shadows.

Zeb handed out food and supplies. "Who wants free grub?"

Ezra was amazed. "Who are you people? I mean, you're not thieves, exactly."

Sabine smiled. "We're not 'exactly' anything. We're a crew. A team. In some ways, a family."

Ezra nodded. Anyone who was against the Empire was okay in his book. But he still wasn't sure he could trust these rebels.

Back on board the *Ghost*, Kanan told the team that they had a new mission. A shady crime boss named Vizago had given them important information.

"Vizago acquired the flight plan for an Imperial transport ship full of Wookiee prisoners."

Ezra protested. He didn't want to go on some crazy rescue mission! But there was no time to take Ezra back to Capital City. He would have to go with them.

Hera piloted the *Ghost* to the Imperial transport's coordinates. Stealthily, she brought their ship up alongside the transport. Kanan, Zeb, and Sabine sneaked aboard while Hera and Ezra remained behind, ready to pilot the *Ghost* out the moment their friends returned.

Kanan nodded to his team. "Okay, you know the plan. Move out."

What the rebels didn't know was that they were walking into a trap. The Wookiees weren't aboard the transport at all.

As Kanan, Zeb, and Sabine crept closer to the transport's brig, a high-ranking Imperial commander named Agent Kallus arrived on board.

An officer updated him. "The rebels are headed for the brig— where quite the surprise awaits."

On board the *Ghost*, Hera couldn't get a message through to Kanan and the others. She realized the *Ghost*'s transmissions were being blocked. The Imperials must have known they were coming!

Hera spun toward Ezra urgently. "You need to board the transport and warn them!"

Ezra couldn't believe what he was hearing. "What? Why don't you do it?"

"I need to be ready to take off, or none of us stands a chance. They need you, Ezra. They need you right now."

Going to warn the others went against everything Ezra had ever learned about fending for himself. But he realized there was no other choice. He sprinted down the halls of the transport ship to find Kanan and the others.

Ezra reached the team just as Kanan was about to open the door to the brig.

Zeb groaned. "Karabast! The kid's blowing another op!"

"It's not an op; it's a trap! Hera sent me to warn you!"

While they were arguing, the brig door slid open, revealing an army of stormtroopers. "RUN!"

Kanan, Ezra, Zeb, and Sabine raced back to the *Ghost*. One by one they jumped in through the ship's air lock.

But just as Ezra was about to follow, Agent Kallus grabbed him! "Ah! Let go!"

The air lock snapped shut. The rebels didn't realize Ezra wasn't on board. In a flash of smoke and engine fire, they took off. Ezra had been left behind.

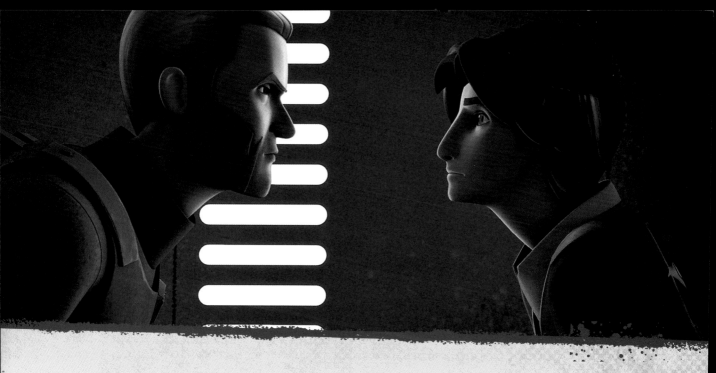

Agent Kallus marched Ezra to a holding cell and shoved him inside. "I am Agent Kallus of the Imperial Security Bureau. And you are?"

Ezra smirked defiantly. "Jabba the Hutt."

Agent Kallus didn't even blink. Ezra sighed. "Look, I just met those guys today. I don't know anything."

Now Agent Kallus did smile. On his face, it was a frightening expression. "You're not here for what you know, 'Jabba.' You're here to be used as bait upon our return to Lothal."

Meanwhile, Kanan and the others realized that Ezra wasn't with them. They had to go back!

Disguising the *Ghost*'s identity signal, Hera piloted it back to the Imperial Star Destroyer that was holding Ezra captive.

Little did they know, Ezra had managed to sneak out of his holding cell! He had nabbed a helmet and was crawling to safety through the ship's air ducts.

On the helmet's intercom, he could hear an Imperial transmission. "I don't know how, but the rebel ship approached without alerting our sensors."

Ezra gasped. "They came back! I don't believe it."

Ezra raced to the air lock, where he saw the rebels waiting for him. Sabine held back the stormtroopers with blaster fire while they all jumped aboard the *Ghost*.

Kanan called to Hera. "Spectre-1 to *Ghost*: we're leaving!"

The *Ghost* zoomed away from the Star Destroyer.

Hera smiled at Ezra when he entered the cockpit. "Welcome aboard. Again."

Ezra looked at the rebels gratefully. "Thank you. I really didn't think you'd come back for me." Then he told them something else he'd heard over the stormtroopers' intercom. Something important.

"I know where they're really taking the Wookiees. Have you heard of the spice mines of Kessel?"

Sabine nodded. "Slaves sent there last a few months, maybe a year."

Ezra looked at each of his new friends. "Then I guess we'd better go save them."

Far away on Kessel, stormtroopers forced handcuffed Wookiees to march into the desert mines. A large laser cannon was positioned on each side of the mine, just in case any daring Wookiees got ideas.

As the Wookiees marched into the dark caverns, dust filled their noses and clung to their fur. A Wookiee child named Kitwarr reached for his father, frightened. But the stormtroopers yanked him away.

Kitwarr's father, Wullffwarro, growled in anger. More than anything, he wanted to attack the trooper and protect his son. But with the handcuffs and cannon blasters, there was nothing he could do.

Suddenly, ash swirled up from the ground around the Wookiees. A dark shadow loomed overhead. Everyone looked up. It was the *Ghost*, coming to the rescue!

Kanan and Sabine used the *Ghost*'s guns to take out the laser cannons. The moment the ship landed, stormtrooper blaster fire broke out everywhere. The Wookiees scattered, confused and frightened. Zeb directed them toward the *Ghost*. "Get in, ya furballs! Now!"

Wullffwarro tried to reach Kitwarr, but a blaster bolt hit him in the shoulder. The dazed Wookiee howled, looking around for Kitwarr. In all the confusion, the little Wookiee had gotten lost!

Ezra realized what was happening and looked frantically for Kitwarr. He spotted him . . . trapped by a stormtrooper on a tall, narrow bridge!

Ezra sped toward Kitwarr, and leaped in front of the little Wookiee, protecting him.

Ezra aimed his energy slingshot at the stormtrooper and knocked him out with three quick blasts! "Gotcha!"

Suddenly, Ezra sensed something behind him and spun around. Agent Kallus was standing at the entrance to the bridge, blocking their path.

Agent Kallus smiled darkly. "It's over."

"Not this time."

Both Ezra and Agent Kallus turned toward the voice. Kanan stood atop the *Ghost* as it flew up beside them. And he was holding a lightsaber—the weapon of a Jedi!

Kallus opened fire on Kanan, but Kanan expertly deflected each shot. One blast glanced off Kanan's lightsaber and hit Kallus's shoulder. The Imperial agent staggered backward and fell over the bridge's railing, where he dangled perilously over the pit below.

Ezra and Kitwarr scampered down the bridge and into the *Ghost*. In a blast of light, the ship took off to safety.

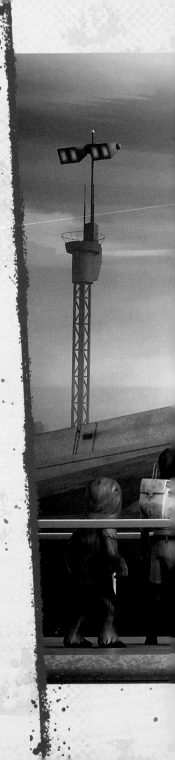

On board the *Ghost*, Kitwarr raced into his father's arms. Wullffwarro howled happily. Then, he turned to Ezra and Kanan, growling more happy sounds.

Sabine translated. "He says if we ever need help, the Wookiees will be there."

The rebels met up with a Wookiee spaceship that would return the former captives to their homes.

Ezra waved good-bye to his new friends. Then he turned to the *Ghost*'s crew. "So . . . I guess you drop me off next?"

Back on Lothal, Ezra had a question for Kanan. As a Jedi, perhaps Kanan could explain the strange intuitions Ezra had sensed his whole life. Ezra asked about an ancient Jedi word. "What's 'the Force'?"

Kanan smiled. "It binds the galaxy together. And it's strong with you, Ezra. Come with me. You can learn what it truly means to be a Jedi."

Ezra thought hard. Joining the rebels would be dangerous, but it might mean having a sort of family for the first time in a long while. A wide grin broke over Ezra's face. To him, that sounded like the best adventure of all.